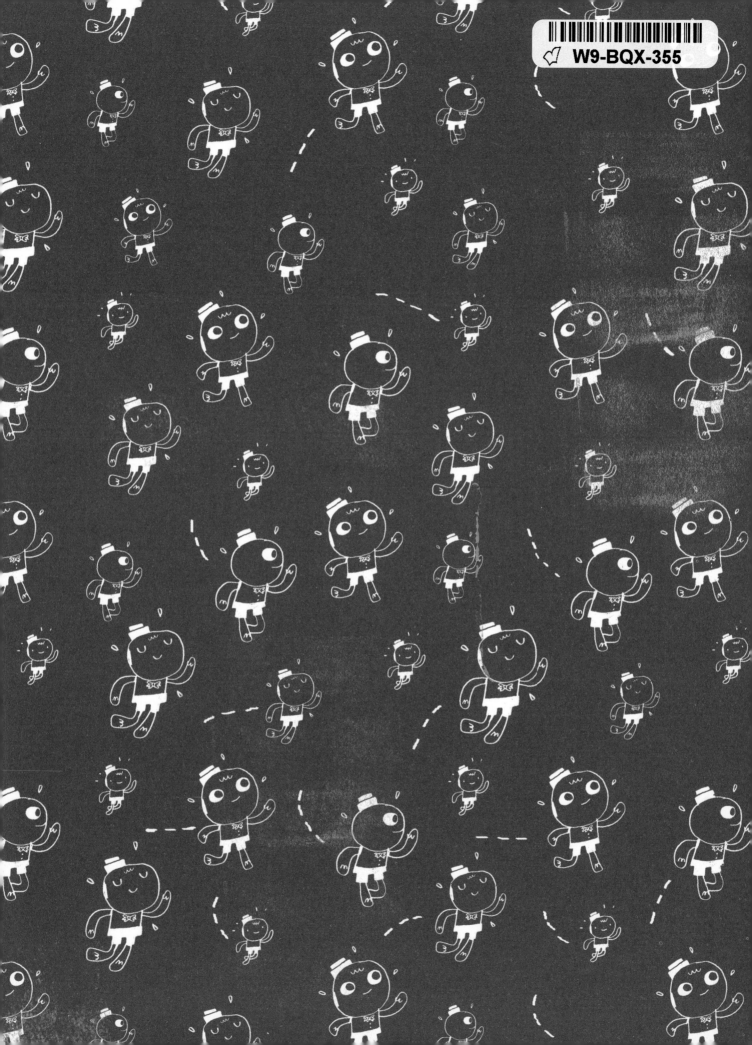

The GINGERBREAD MAN

LOOSE in the SCHOOL

ROOM 103

ROOM 104

COMPUTER LAB

NURSE'S OFFICE

GYMNASIUM

STAIRS

CAFETERIA

Laura Murray · illustrated by **Mike Lowery**

G. P. PUTNAM'S SONS · AN IMPRINT OF PENGUIN GROUP (USA) INC.

To Kyle, Caitlyn, and Bridget—
my three smart cookies.
And to Chris, my co-baker.
—L. M.

This book is dedicated to Allister,
an amazingly awesome daughter.
And thank you to Katrin
for all of her help.
—M. L.

G. P. PUTNAM'S SONS A division of Penguin Young Readers Group.

Published by The Penguin Group. Penguin Group (USA) Inc., 375 Hudson Street, New York, NY 10014, U.S.A. Penguin Group (Canada), 90 Eglinton Avenue East, Suite 700, Toronto, Ontario M4P 2Y3, Canada (a division of Pearson Penguin Canada Inc.). Penguin Books Ltd, 80 Strand, London WC2R 0RL, England. Penguin Ireland, 25 St. Stephen's Green, Dublin 2, Ireland (a division of Penguin Books Ltd.). Penguin Group (Australia), 250 Camberwell Road, Camberwell, Victoria 3124, Australia (a division of Pearson Australia Group Pty Ltd). Penguin Books India Pvt Ltd, 11 Community Centre, Panchsheel Park, New Delhi - 110 017, India. Penguin Group (NZ), 67 Apollo Drive, Rosedale, North Shore 0632, New Zealand (a division of Pearson New Zealand Ltd). Penguin Books (South Africa) (Pty) Ltd, 24 Sturdee Avenue, Rosebank, Johannesburg 2196, South Africa. Penguin Books Ltd, Registered Offices: 80 Strand, London WC2R 0RL, England.

Text copyright © 2011 by Laura Murray. Illustrations copyright © 2011 by Mike Lowery.

Design by Ryan Thomann. Text set in Bokka and Dr. Eric, with a bit of hand-lettering.
The illustrations were rendered with pencil, traditional screen printing, and digital color.

Library of Congress Cataloging-in-Publication Data
Murray, Laura, 1970- The gingerbread man loose in the school / Laura Murray ; illustrated by Mike Lowery.
p. cm. Summary: A gingerbread man searches all over the school for the group of children that made him and then left him behind. [1. Stories in rhyme. 2. Cookies—Fiction. 3. Schools—Fiction.] I. Lowery, Mike, 1980- ill. II. Title. PZ8.3.M9368Gi 2011 [E]—dc22 2009006642
ISBN 978-0-399-25052-1 11

FINALLY, I thought, **I'M A GINGERBREAD MAN!**

I picked up my **toe**

and I hopped down the **hall,**

then into a room
that was tidy and small.

NURSE

The **nurse** came right over.
She squatted down **low.**

I **pointed** and showed her
my broken-off **toe.**

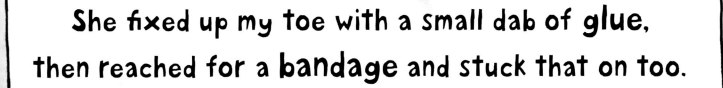

She fixed up my toe with a small dab of glue,
then reached for a **bandage** and stuck that on too.

With **spectacular** speed,
I slid to the floor

and bounded right in
through a large wooden **door.**

I **leapt**
for a table,

but landed **inside**
a brown paper bag
with its top
open **wide.**

I tried to climb out, but I spied two big **eyes**.

They **peered** in the bag with a look of surprise.

I'LL SKIP AND I'LL SKIP,
AS FAST AS I CAN.
I CAN CATCH THEM! I'M THEIR
GINGERBREAD
MAN!

I passed through an **office**,

slipped under a **door**,

and discovered a **room** I had yet to **explore**.

PRINCIPAL

I jumped on a desk,

then **leapt** to a **chair**.

It started to **spin**
and I twirled through the **air**.

WEEEE!

Despite feeling dizzy,
I jumped up for **more**,
but **froze** when I saw
someone peek in the **door**.

And there on the wall was a drawing of me!

The poster said:

MISSING

FROM ROOM 23

IF FOUND, PLEASE RETURN HIM AS SOON AS YOU CAN. WE THINK HE IS LOST, HE'S OUR GINGERBREAD MAN.